W9-BAP-952

MULBERRY BOOKS

JACK'S GARDEN

HENRY COLE

HENRY COLE

JACK'S GARDEN

GREENWILLOW BOOKS, NEW YORK

FOR BIWI, SPANKY, DEMMY, AND TISHY

The full-color art was created with colored pencils on paper of different colors. The text type is Garamond.

Jack's Garden
Copyright © 1995 by Henry Cole. All rights reserved. Printed in the United States of America.
www.harperchildrens.com

Library of Congress Cataloging-in-Publication Data
Cole, Henry. Jack's garden/by Henry Cole.
 p. cm. "Greenwillow Books."
Summary: Cumulative text and illustrations depict what happens in Jack's garden after he plants his seeds.
[1. Gardening—Fiction.] I. Title.
PZ7.C67345Jac 1995 [E]—dc20
94—6249 CIP AC

ISBN 0-688-13501-3 (trade)
ISBN 0-688-15283-X (pbk.)

For information address HarperCollins Children's Books, a division of HarperCollins Publishers, 195 Broadway, New York, NY 10007.
First Edition
22 23 24 25 PC 20 19

GARDEN CLAW

PRUNING SHEARS

This is the garden

that Jack planted.

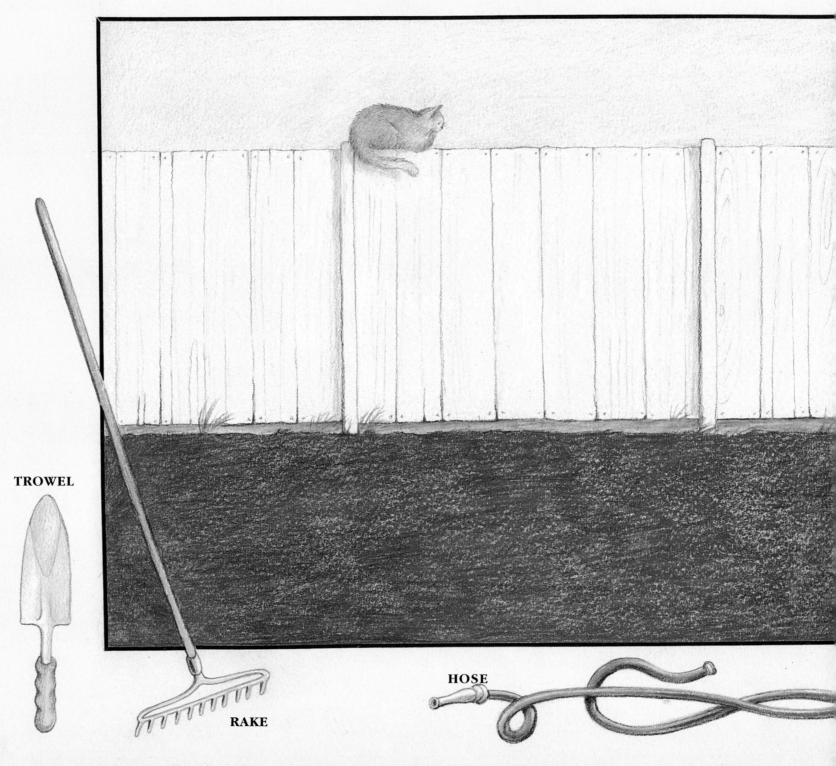

TROWEL

RAKE

HOSE

SHOVEL

HOE

WATERING
CAN

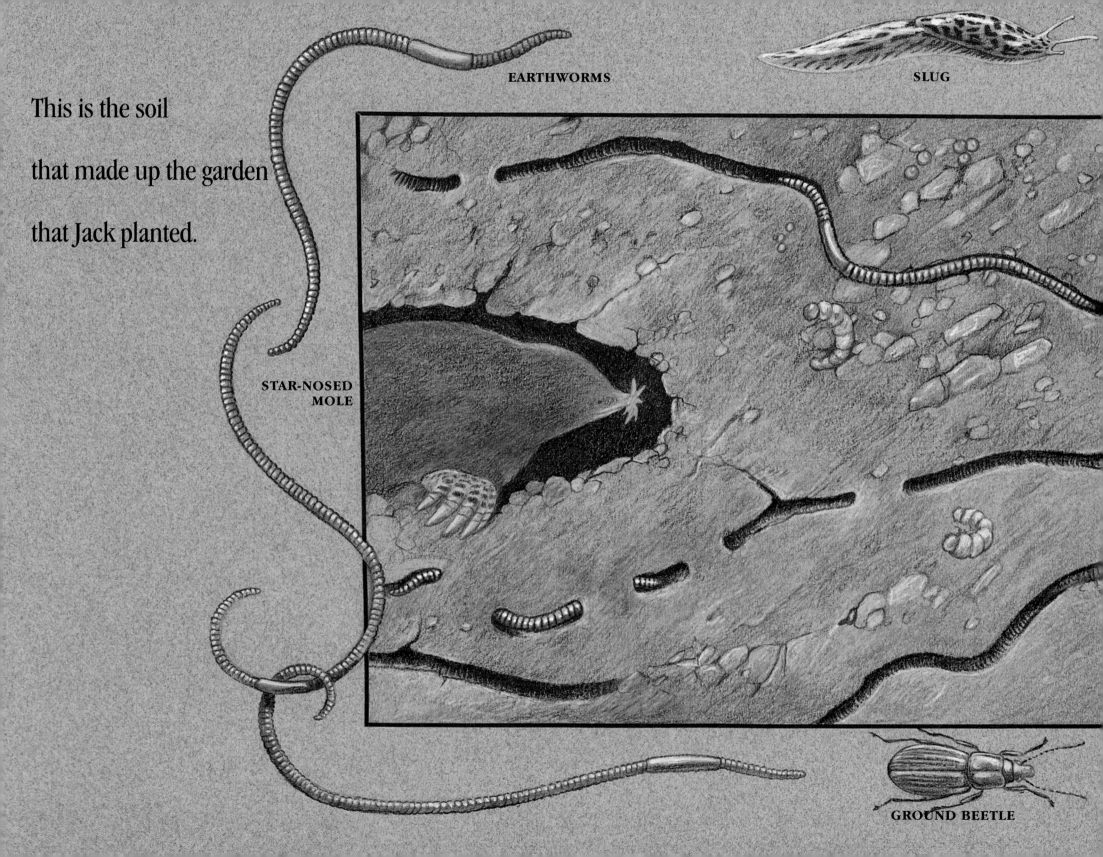

This is the soil

that made up the garden

that Jack planted.

EARTHWORMS

SLUG

STAR-NOSED
MOLE

GROUND BEETLE

FLY PUPA

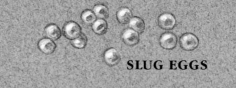
BEETLE LARVA

SLUG EGGS

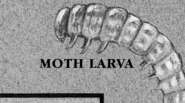
MOTH LARVA

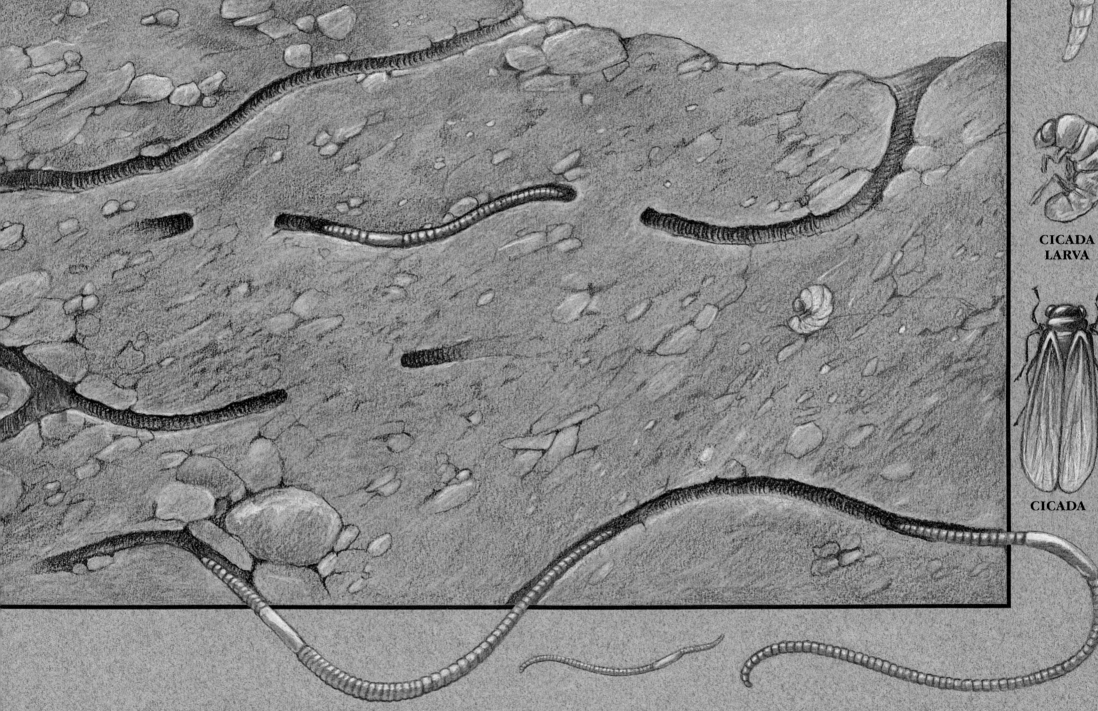
CICADA LARVA

CICADA

These are the seeds

that fell on the soil

that made up the garden

that Jack planted.

LUPINE SEEDS

PHLOX SEEDS

DIANTHUS SEEDS

POPPY SEEDS

HOLLYHOCK SEEDS

SUNFLOWER SEEDS

MILKWEED SEEDS

BLUET WILDFLOWER 95¢

ALLIUM

YARROW

WILDFLOWER MIX 75¢

LUPINE FLOWER SEED

COREOPSIS

MORNING GLORY

DAISIES

This is the rain

that wet the seeds

that fell on the soil

that made up the garden

that Jack planted.

STRATUS
CLOUD

CIRRUS
CLOUD

CIRROCUMULUS
CLOUD

RAIN
GAUGE

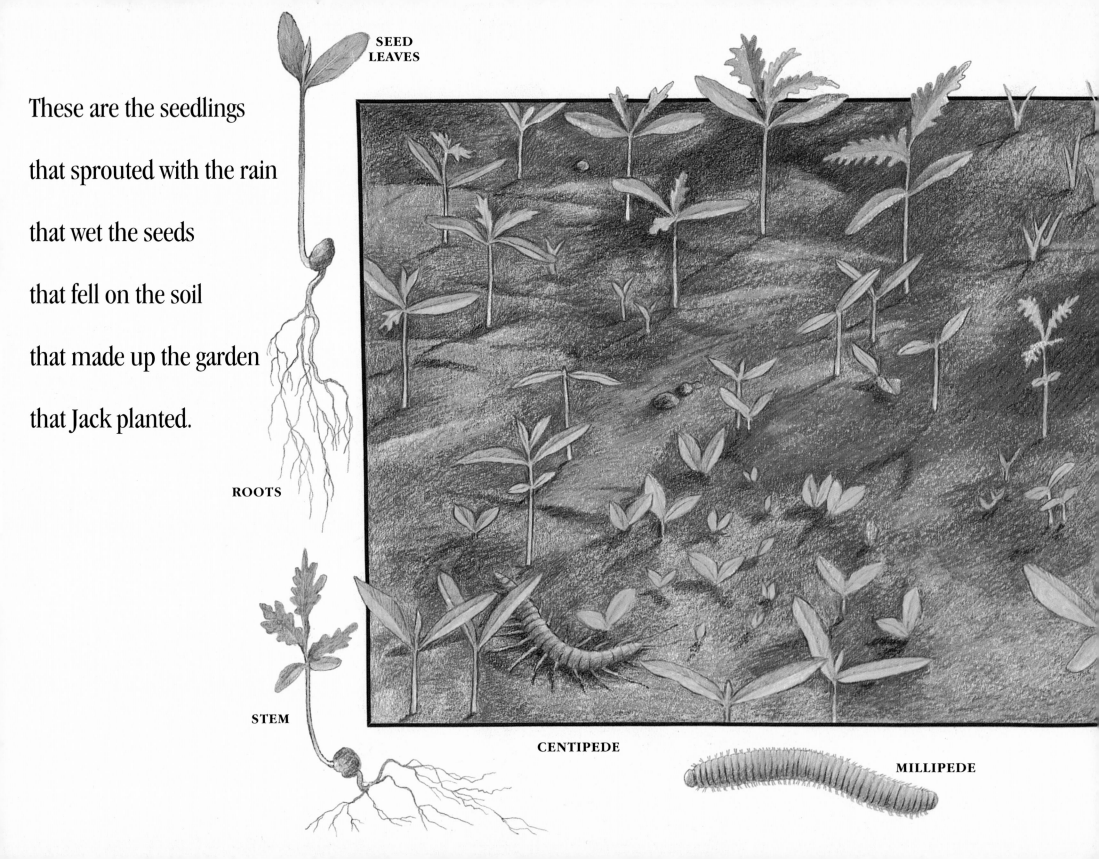

These are the seedlings

that sprouted with the rain

that wet the seeds

that fell on the soil

that made up the garden

that Jack planted.

SEED
LEAVES

ROOTS

STEM

CENTIPEDE

MILLIPEDE

ADULT
LEAVES

ROBIN

SEED
LEAVES

ROOTS

SOW BUG

GERMINATING
SEED

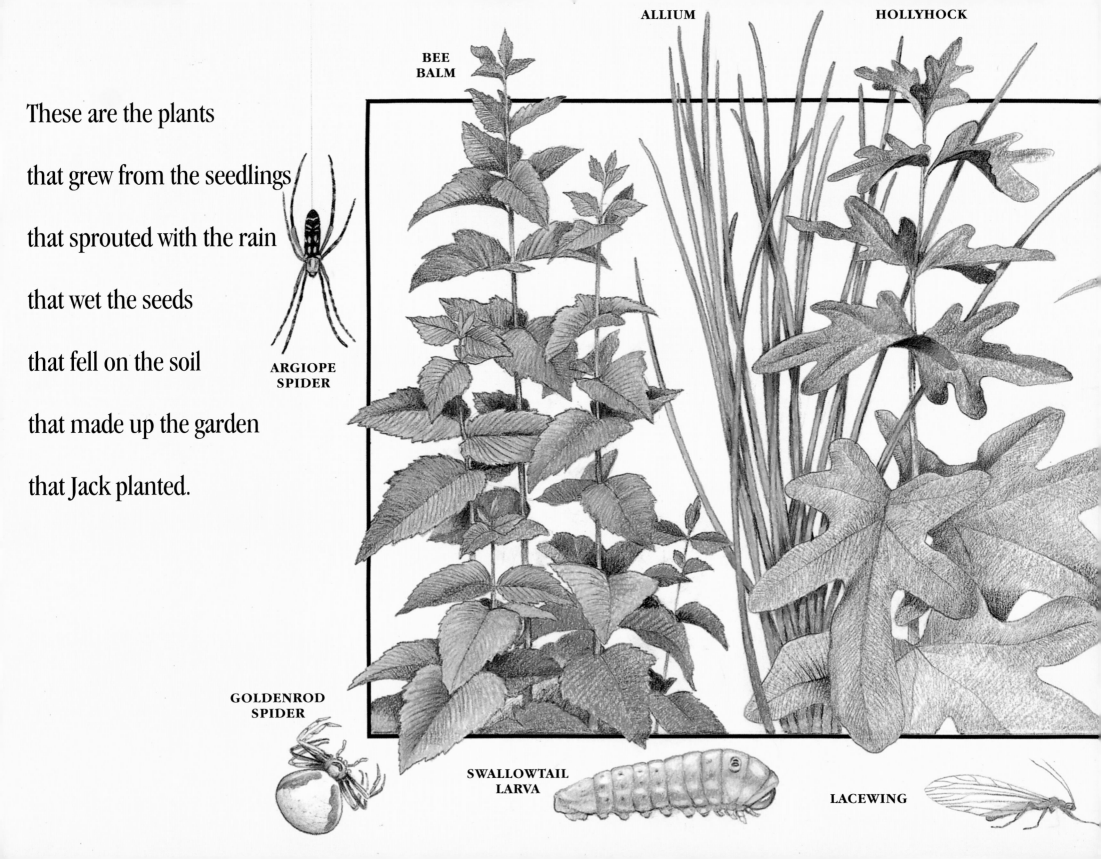

These are the plants

that grew from the seedlings

that sprouted with the rain

that wet the seeds

that fell on the soil

that made up the garden

that Jack planted.

ALLIUM

HOLLYHOCK

BEE
BALM

ARGIOPE
SPIDER

GOLDENROD
SPIDER

SWALLOWTAIL
LARVA

LACEWING

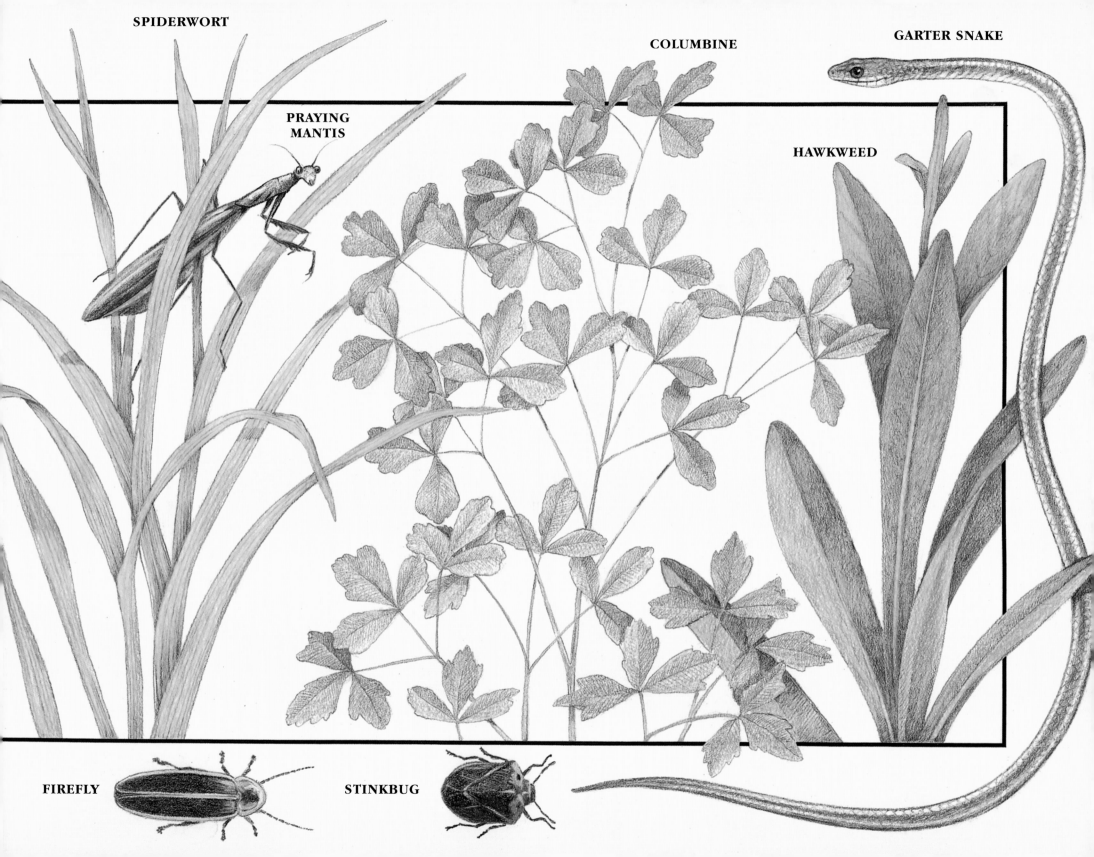

SPIDERWORT

PRAYING MANTIS

COLUMBINE

GARTER SNAKE

HAWKWEED

FIREFLY

STINKBUG

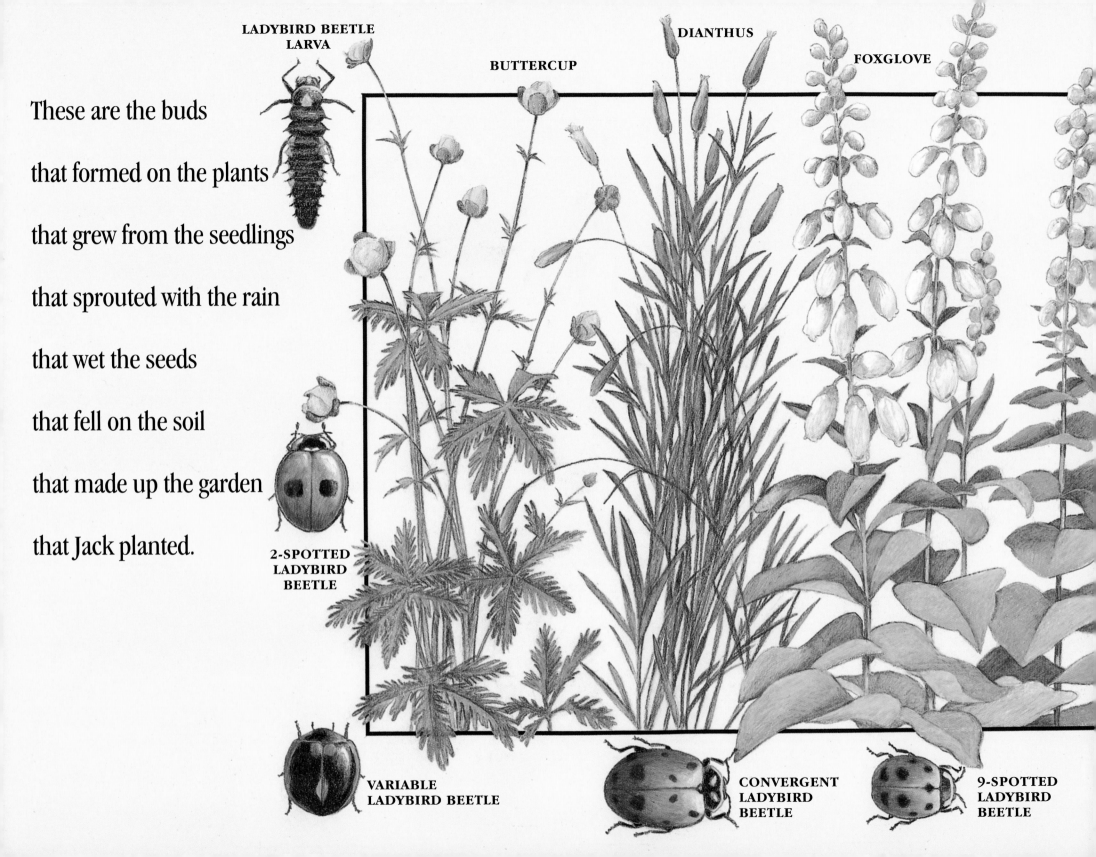

These are the buds

that formed on the plants

that grew from the seedlings

that sprouted with the rain

that wet the seeds

that fell on the soil

that made up the garden

that Jack planted.

LADYBIRD BEETLE
LARVA

BUTTERCUP

DIANTHUS

FOXGLOVE

2-SPOTTED
LADYBIRD
BEETLE

VARIABLE
LADYBIRD BEETLE

CONVERGENT
LADYBIRD
BEETLE

9-SPOTTED
LADYBIRD
BEETLE

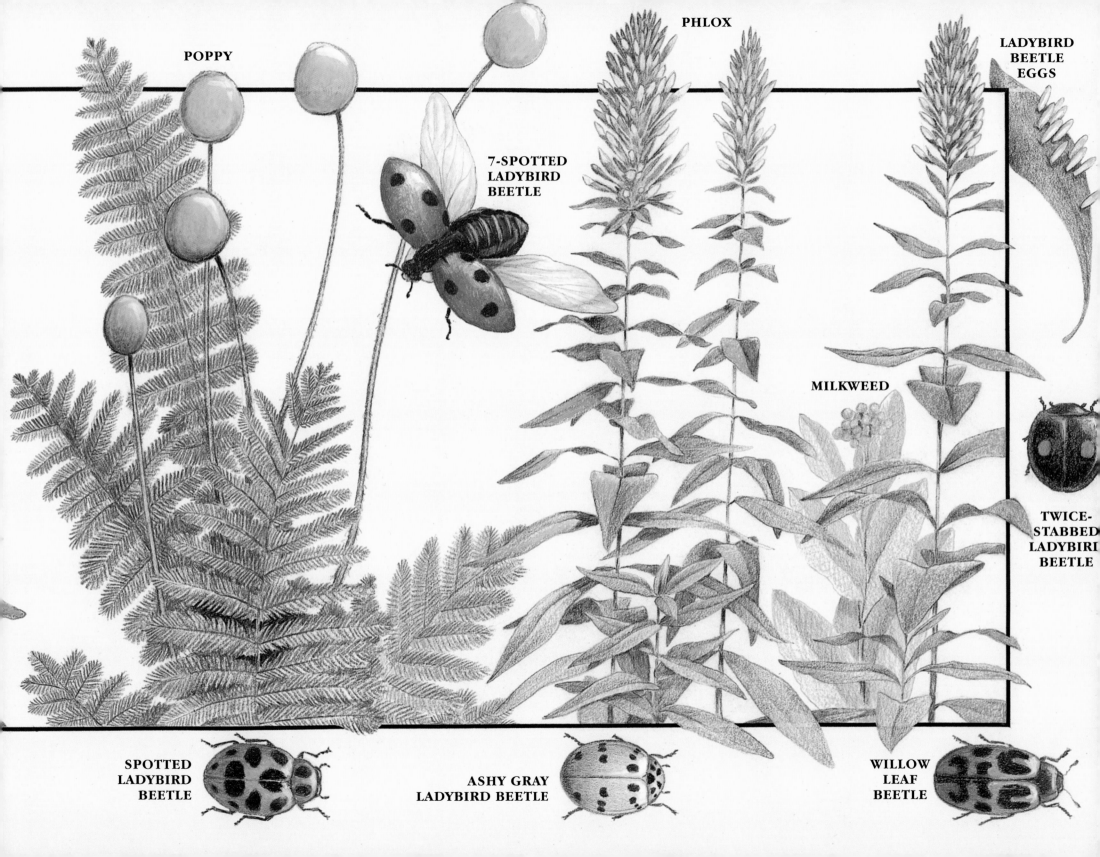

POPPY

PHLOX

LADYBIRD BEETLE EGGS

7-SPOTTED LADYBIRD BEETLE

MILKWEED

TWICE-STABBED LADYBIRD BEETLE

SPOTTED LADYBIRD BEETLE

ASHY GRAY LADYBIRD BEETLE

WILLOW LEAF BEETLE

These are the flowers

that blossomed from the buds

that formed on the plants

that grew from the seedlings

that sprouted with the rain

that wet the seeds

that fell on the soil

that made up the garden

that Jack planted.

ASTER

BLACK-EYED SUSAN

LUPINE

RED CLOVER

WHITE CLOVER

FLEABANE

WILD GERANIUM

YARROW

MULLEIN

COREOPSIS

BEE
BALM

PINKS

BLUET

SPIDERWORT

DAISY

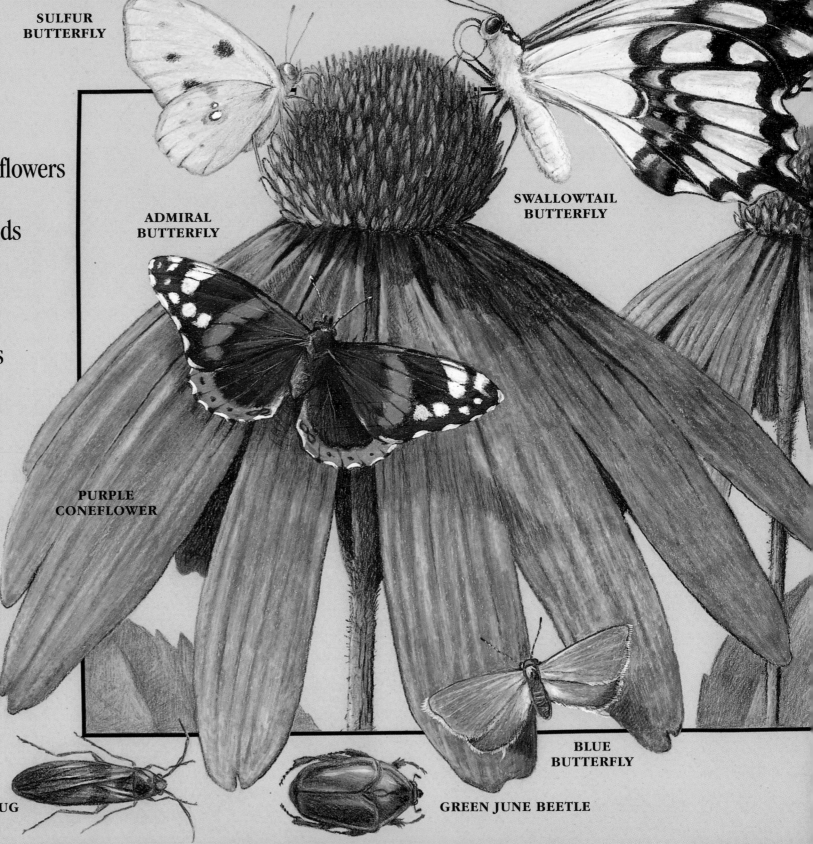

These are the insects

that sipped nectar from the flowers

that blossomed from the buds

that formed on the plants

that grew from the seedlings

that sprouted with the rain

that wet the seeds

that fell on the soil

that made up the garden

that Jack planted.

SULFUR
BUTTERFLY

SWALLOWTAIL
BUTTERFLY

ADMIRAL
BUTTERFLY

PURPLE
CONEFLOWER

BLUE
BUTTERFLY

MILKWEED BUG

GREEN JUNE BEETLE

SOLDIER BEETLE

SKIPPER BUTTERFLY

SARA ORANGE TIP
BUTTERFLY

BUMBLEBEE

BUCKEYE
BUTTERFLY

LONG-HORNED BEETLE

COPPER BUTTERFLY

METALLIC
BEE

These are the birds

that chased the insects

that sipped nectar from the flowers

that blossomed from the buds

that formed on the plants

that grew from the seedlings

that sprouted with the rain

that wet the seeds

that fell on the soil

that made up the garden

that Jack planted.

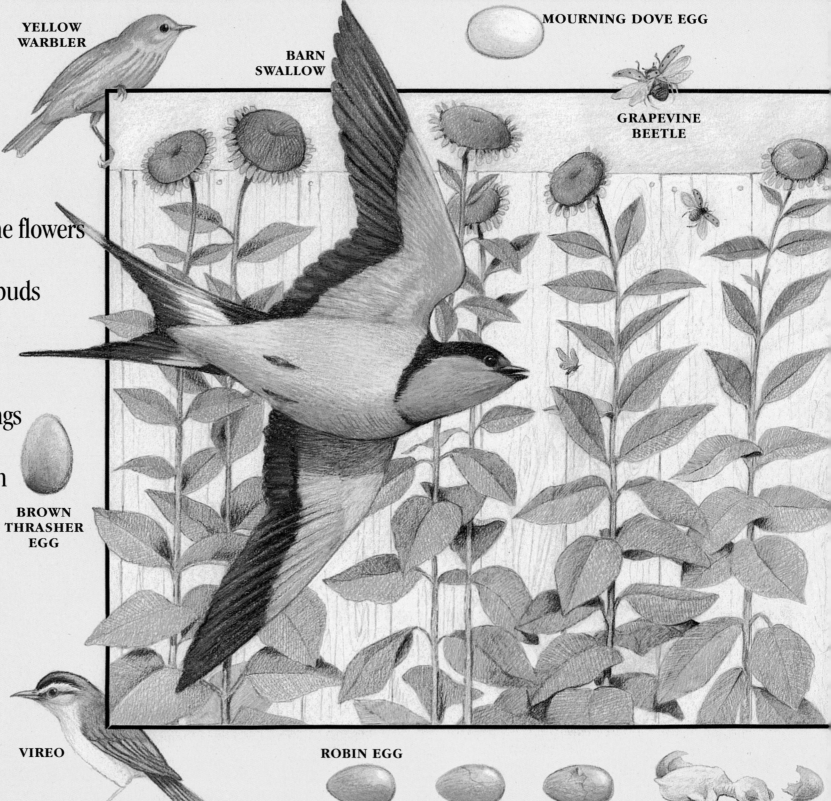

YELLOW
WARBLER

BARN
SWALLOW

MOURNING DOVE EGG

GRAPEVINE
BEETLE

BROWN
THRASHER
EGG

VIREO

ROBIN EGG

YELLOW
WARBLER EGG

GOLDFINCH EGG

CATBIRD

SUNFLOWERS

VIREO
EGG

BLUEBIRD
EGG

BLUEBIRD

BARN
SWALLOW
EGG

CATBIRD EGG

GOLDFINCH

MORNING GLORY

MOURNING DOVE

And this is the garden

that Jack planted.

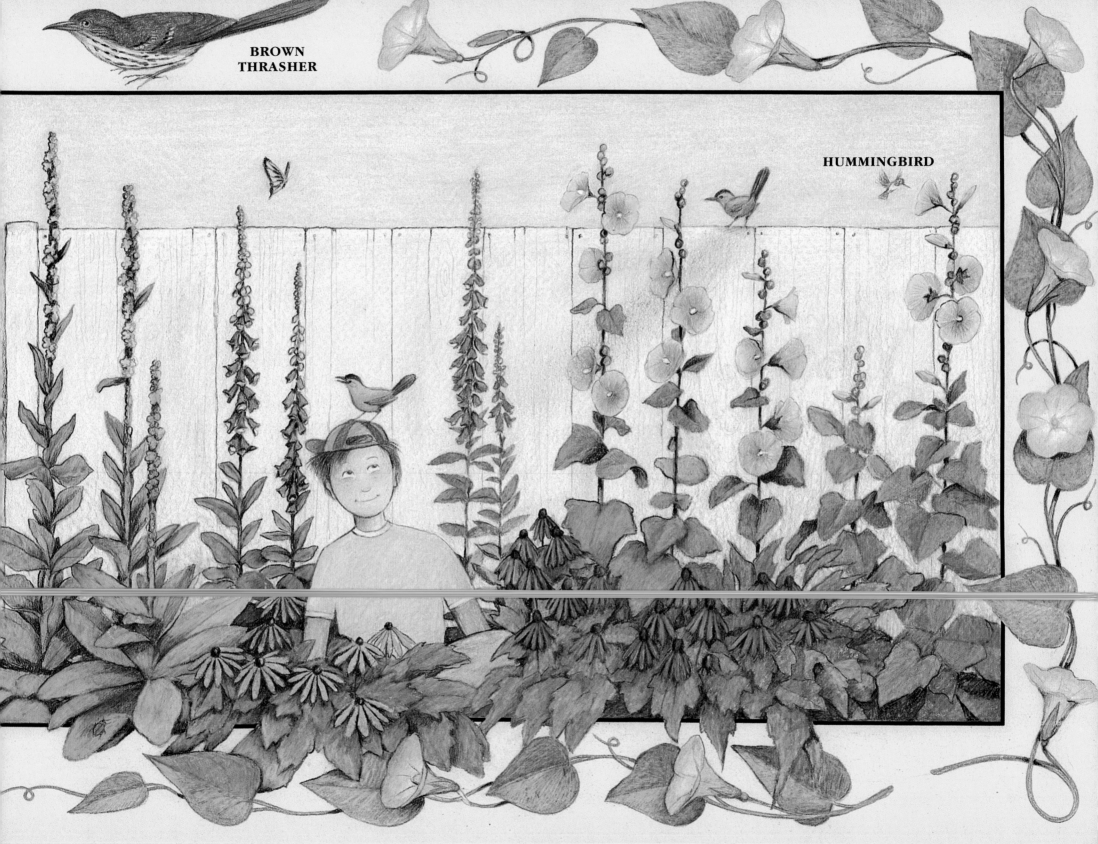

BROWN
THRASHER

HUMMINGBIRD

TO START YOUR OWN GARDEN,

find a spot where you may dig. Your mom or dad may need to help you get started. Choose a place that gets some sunshine and isn't too wet.

Hardware stores and supermarkets sell all kinds of seeds. Or you can order seeds through the mail: Try W. Atlee Burpee Seed Company (300 Park Avenue, Warminster, PA 18974) or Park Seed Company (Cokesbury Road, Greenwood, SC 29647).

The seeds you get may be very delicate, so handle them carefully. They shouldn't be planted deeply in the soil. Here's a good way to plant very tiny seeds, like poppy seeds: Put some soil in a bowl or pan and gently mix the seeds in with it. Then scatter the seeded soil over the ground. After planting or scattering the seeds, water them gently.

(Or maybe you'll be lucky like Jack and have a spring shower do the watering!)

Some plants like sunnier spots, some like shadier places. Look at the backs of the seed packets to find out which are best for different parts of your garden. Black-eyed Susans, for example, like it nice and sunny. Spiderwort likes it shady and moist.

Some plants are tall, some are short. Most of the time the seed packet will tell you how tall that plant will become. Put tall plants at the back of your garden and short ones up front.

Some plants bloom in the spring, like foxglove, and some later in the summer, like hollyhocks. You can grow different kinds of plants so that something will be blooming all season.

A good place to get more information on starting a garden is your local County Extension Office or your library.

Happy Gardening!